P[
Cl

'Turn the world over and if you...
The way to the treasure you're certain to find...'

Clancy's cabin is a wonderful place for Skip, Timothy and Marina to spend a camping holiday.

It is high summer, when the days are blue and warm, ideal for swimming, for camp fires and adventuring – and for treasure hunting.

When the children find a clue to hidden treasure they think at first that their father has hidden it for them to find. After all, he's always playing jokes on them. But *is* it a joke this time?

Other books by Margaret Mahy

MARGARET MAHY

Clancy's Cabin

Illustrated by Trevor Stubley

Puffin Books

PUFFIN BOOKS

Published by the Penguin Group
27 Wrights Lane, London W8 5TZ, England
Viking Penguin Inc., 40 West 23rd Street, New York, New York 10010, USA
Penguin Books Australia Ltd, Ringwood, Victoria, Australia
Penguin Books Canada Ltd, 2801 John Street, Markham, Ontario, Canada L3R 1B4
Penguin Books (NZ) Ltd, 182–190 Wairau Road, Auckland 10, New Zealand

Penguin Books Ltd, Registered Offices: Harmondsworth, Middlesex, England

First published by J. M. Dent and Sons 1977
Published in Puffin Books 1987
10 9 8 7 6 5 4

Printed and bound in Great Britain by
Cox & Wyman Ltd, Reading

Contents

I

Mr Harrington's Joke

Mr Harrington was a man who was fond of a joke. In fact he liked laughing so much that his face was covered in smile lines all the time, and his blue eyes were either getting ready for the next laugh, or still remembering the last one. That was the sort of man he was. Mrs Harrington would say, "Really, I don't know whether I've got four children or five", meaning that Mr Harrington was like one of the children himself, with all his tricks and teases.

The real children of the house were Esmond (who was always called Skip), Marina, Timothy and William (who was only two years old and known as Little Beetle). You can see there were a lot of them, and what with the giggling and games, the fighting, the laughing and Mr Harrington's jokes, there was never very much stillness around the Harrington house. It would have worried the neighbours, if there had been any neighbours, but the Harrington family with all its lively children lived in New Zealand, in a big, old farmhouse in the country, and the nearest neighbours were well out of worrying distance. From their house the children could see trees and sky and lots and lots of gentle green hills, for they lived in a valley and the hills shut out the rest of the world.

Every day Mr Harrington got into his car and drove to work in the city twelve miles away.

"It's a long way," he would say, "but it's worth it to come home to the valley again."

The three older children went to a little school, but in the holidays they had only each other to play with so perhaps it was just as well there were several children in the Harrington family. They were rather alike to look at, though Marina being a girl had long hair. In fact, it was long enough to wear in plaits. The difficulty was that she was always losing her ribbons and then it all came undone and got knots in it.

8

"Why can't I have it cut off short like Skip's and Timmy's?" she used to grumble as she brushed it angrily, tugging at its tangles. "It's not even as if it was all golden and lovely. It's just blackish-brownish and ordinary."

However, at school she was proud of being the only girl with plaits, and glad her mother did not take her seriously and have it cut off. Skip's hair curled which meant he had tangles too, and as for Timothy's—his stood up in a funny, tufty way which made him look like some curious, crested bird. Nobody could make it lie flat for long. All the children had blue eyes like their father (though Skip was most like him of all, which was funny because he was quite different in character and ways of thinking), and in the summer they looked very brown indeed . . . not just their hair, but their faces and legs and arms and backs. Timothy used to get freckly as well.

Skip, the eldest, was eleven, Marina was ten, Timothy was eight. Perhaps because he was the eldest Skip always seemed to take things more seriously than either Marina or Timothy, who were always giggling and teasing and trying to get out of the jobs they were given to do around the house. It wasn't that Skip didn't enjoy himself just as much as they did, but he was often quieter and more thoughtful about it, and whenever he remembered he really tried to be helpful. But, in spite of these small differences, all three of them loved cooking over campfires, making houses in trees, catching eels in the creek and other noisy, messy, wonderful games. Little Beetle, of course, was too small.

"Plenty of children and plenty of rackety clack," Mr Harrington would say when people asked him what his house was like.

Then in the Christmas holidays, just after New Year, Mrs Harrington had a new baby. Mr Harrington's sister, who was almost as full of jokes as he was, came to look after the children.

"My word, another boy!" said Mr Harrington at tea. "Your mother must have felt it was getting too quiet around here." He grinned to himself as if he had said something very funny, and winked at Aunt Helen, who started laughing too.

"What's funny, Daddy?" asked Marina. But their father just went on grinning and looking very pleased with himself without saying anything more.

"Something's making Daddy laugh," Skip said after tea to Marina and Timothy. "He's got a joke on and he's not telling us. He's got that look in his eye. We'd better watch him pretty carefully."

Sometimes Mr Harrington's jokes worried Skip. When he told the boys at school about them, they always looked a little surprised at the thought of a father behaving in such a way. It made Skip feel proud of his father, and yet uncertain of him too, so he always tried to guess what Mr Harrington was going to do before he did it. That way the surprise wouldn't be

too great. Marina and Timothy, on the other hand, did not seem to mind having such an unexpected sort of father at all, but of course they couldn't help trying to guess his jokes too, just for the fun of it.

So they all watched their father very closely indeed, when they remembered to. He was remarkably pleased with life, and just before their mother came home he took three days off work. Some of the time he spent around the house painting the kitchen as a surprise for Mrs Harrington.

"Is this your joke, Dad? I know you've got a joke on," Skip asked him.

"A joke, Skip?" Mr Harrington said, carefully painting around a ledge. "I'm far too busy to joke." But this was not at all true, because Mr Harrington was never too busy to joke. He was not at home all the time either. For a day and a half he quite vanished from sight and they knew he hadn't gone to town because he was still wearing his old painty clothes when he came back. He wouldn't tell them where he had been, and neither would Aunt Helen.

At last that bright and special day arrived—the day when Mother was coming home. All the world seemed blue and gold and green, with sky, sun and hills. It was a *best* day, a warm, glad day, and the children felt warm and glad too, as they put on their best clothes specially to match the morning. Mr Harrington, Aunt Helen and Little Beetle set out to collect Mother.

"Now, Skip, you're in charge," cried Mr Harrington. "Keep out of the house because it's tidy, don't dirty yourselves or I'll skin you, and keep away from the elephants." Of course, there weren't any elephants, but Mr Harrington had to have his joke. He just couldn't help it.

It was hard and long waiting . . . hard to keep still, hard to keep tidy, but at last, small and determined, they saw the car coming back down the road. Trees hid it for a moment, and then it appeared again, pulling up the hill with a grinding noise. Yes, it was their own car with Aunt Helen driving, and there in the back were Daddy and Mother looking out, very happy to see their children bobbing up and down with excitement like flowers in the wind.

Skip pulled the gate open and the car swept grandly in. In a moment Mother was out of the car. Her arms were open to them and they all ran to hug her, even Skip who was eleven. They hugged and hugged each other lots of times and said, "Gosh, we've missed you!" over and over again.

Then Mr Harrington, behind them, said, "Aren't you going to say hallo to your new brother?"

They turned around. There stood Mr Harrington with a huge smile almost cutting his face in half and he had *two* babies—one on each arm.

All the children shouted out together, "Two babies! two!"

"Are they both ours, both, Mummy? Both?" yelled Timothy, pulling his mother's skirt.

Mrs Harrington looked from the children's surprised faces to Mr Harrington's laughing one. "Didn't your rascal of a father tell you?" she said. "We've got little twins."

Then she made Mr Harrington show them the babies, two little boys with tiny, red, crumpled, sleeping faces and each with a sprinkling of brown hair.

"This one is Adam and this one is Oliver," said Mr Harrington.

"Well, the joke's on you this time," Mrs Harrington told him. "You've got them the wrong way round."

"Aren't they darlings?" Marina cried. "Can we hold them?"

"In a minute, dears," Mrs Harrington said as she went into the house . . . and when she saw the newly painted kitchen, well, it was her turn to be very surprised indeed. Then she said a funny thing.

"What about the children? Have you told them about . . .?"

"Shhh! Shhh!" hissed Mr Harrington, shaking his head quickly.

Skip looked at his father closely. "You've still got a joke on," he said accusingly. "What is it?"

"Now, Skip, you know I'm too busy to joke," Mr Harrington replied. Then suddenly he began to laugh and laugh, and although they didn't know why he was laughing all the family joined in, because why, because it was such a lovely day and it was so wonderful to have Mother home and new little twin brothers.

What they forgot was that Mr Harrington's joke was still going on, and that there was more to come.

2
The Joke Goes On

In the next day or two it became plain that the Harrington house was going to be noisier than ever before. Suddenly everybody seemed to be stepping on everybody else.

"I told you so!" said Mr Harrington to Mother and Aunt Helen, but what he had told them he did not say. Adam and Oliver cried whenever they were hungry, and it seemed that they were always hungry. When they weren't crying everyone else had to be quiet. Skip, Marina, Timothy and Little Beetle weren't used to being quiet.

"What did I say?" Mr Harrington cried triumphantly. "It isn't the children's fault. We'll have to try my plan." But he wouldn't tell them what his plan was.

16

Fortunately the days were blue and summery and the children bounced around outside, getting browner and browner and more and more scratched and tangled. However, sometimes they had to come inside, and then everyone seemed to tumble over them and say, "For goodness' sake, get out of the way."

That was how it was until one day Mr Harrington rang the big cowbell that called his children to stop whatever they were doing and to come at once. The children scrambled in from all directions.

"My word!" cried Mr Harrington. "You look like a tribe of Indians. Is Marina wearing a bird's nest on her head, or is it just that she hasn't brushed her hair this morning?" He sighed sadly. "What's the use of having a daughter if she is going to turn herself into a walking haystack whenever she can? I might just as well have stuck to boys."

Marina grinned, because she could see her father wasn't really cross. "It's the wind, Daddy," she said. "My hair gets all tangly." Mr Harrington was already talking about something else.

"I've packed a bite to eat in the car," he said, "and I'm going to take you ruffians and your mother for a drive to Clancy's cabin—just for afternoon tea and look-round. Your aunt will keep an eye on Little Beetle and the twin-ohs."

With these words he packed them into the car, and off they went into the sunny day, very pleased at the thought of a drive to their favourite picnic place.

17

In about ten minutes they turned off the road, going bounce, bounce across two paddocks. They were now going over a farm belonging to Clancy O'Reagan, an old friend of Mr Harrington's and, as usual, Mr Harrington began to tell the children what a wonderful time he and Clancy had had, when they were boys.

"My word," he said, "those were the days. Clancy's father owned the place then, of course. We used to camp out all over the holidays—campfires, damming up the creek to make swimming pools . . . we did everything you could think of. And the treasure hunts! My grandfather used to arrange wonderful treasure hunts for us, all over the valley, and off we'd set, Clancy and I, on our ponies searching out the clues . . . my word!" He shook his head slowly, lost in the glory of past days.

When Mr Harrington was a boy he had lived with his grandfather in the very farmhouse the family lived in now. Though his grandfather died and his mother had to sell the house and go and live in the city, Mr Harrington did not forget the holidays with Clancy, or stop loving the country. Years later, when he was married, he saw in the papers that his grandfather's old house was for sale again. He had saved up a lot of money by then and he took it all out of the bank, and Mrs Harrington took all her money out too, and they bought the old house—just like that.

Clancy was still there living on his old farm, just the same as ever. He had no children which was a pity, because Mr Harrington and Clancy spent a lot of time visiting each other and laughing over old jokes no one else could see the fun of, and it would have been nice if there had been some O'Reagan children to play with.

Thinking of the camping and the treasure hunts Mr Harrington had enjoyed as a boy, Marina said wistfully,

"I'd love to go treasure hunting on a pony. I wish we could."

"I wish we could just go camping!" Timothy yelled, his eyes shining. "I'd love that!" As Timothy spoke, Skip saw his father's face in the car mirror grinning delightedly at some secret thought.

"Why are you smiling, Dad?" he asked.

"Just a happy memory, Skip, just a happy memory," Mr Harrington replied. "There's Mrs Clancy in her garden. Give her a wave, kids."

They all waved and shouted to the little figure bent over the pea rows, and Mrs Clancy stood up and waved back as they sailed past her house and garden, coming at last to their picnic place.

The paddock sloped away in a long shallow gully filled with bush and gorse, and bare grassy patches where the sun fell hot and golden just asking someone to picnic there. Clancy let them come here as often as they liked, and if they wanted to they could go up to the house and Mrs Clancy gave them fresh milk, and fruit from the orchard.

In the shade of some twisted native fuchsia trees stood a funny old two-roomed hut, looking as if it

19

had sprouted out of the ground along with the grass and the trees themselves. It was made of wood, half rusty with lichen, half green with moss, and big ferns grew high under its windows. The sun was hot on the grass, and through the gorse the stream sparkled and beckoned the children, but Mr Harrington said, "My word, we used to have a great time in that cabin when we were boys . . . I remember Clancy's father building it for us . . . we felt like a couple of kings camping there. Let's have lunch inside with the spiders, shall we?"

"Not on a lovely day!" cried Marina. "It's pretty wet and dirty in the hut."

"It's much better outside," begged Timothy.

But Mr Harrington was determined. "It's lovely in the summer time," he said. "The damp will make it all the cooler. Don't disappoint the spiders. They love to see a few children around." He marched off taking the food with him, quite ignoring the sunshine and the call of the little stony creek. His family could do nothing but follow him. He turned the squeaky handle and pushed the door open.

"Good gracious!" he cried. "What on earth has been going on here?"

The children crowded in to look and their mouths fell open with surprise. Instead of the dirty, dark little room they had expected to see, they saw a room newly lined and smelling of fresh blue and white paint. Some-one had put in cupboards made of old boxes, and built seats and a table against one wall. And someone—no doubt the same someone—had washed the windows, put up blue curtains and set a fern in a pot on each window-sill. In the next room they caught glimpses of bunks and of a sheepskin rug on the floor.

"My word," said Mr Harrington marching in and looking round, "this looks a wonderful place for three children to have a camping holiday, doesn't it?"

He looked at Mrs Harrington, who had been very quiet all the way there. But now she smiled and said, "Yes, it does look lovely."

"A camping holiday? Us?" cried Skip, finding his voice suddenly.

Mr Harrington looked at them with his head on one side.

"Don't you like the idea?" he asked.

"It's wonderful!" Skip yelled. "Isn't it, you kids? Are we allowed?"

"Oh please, Daddy!" said Marina, pulling his arm anxiously.

"Please!" echoed Timothy, sounding quite fierce as he said it.

Mr Harrington began to unpack the food basket. "Well, you see," he said, "here we are with twins. We weren't expecting two babies and you know how busy your mother and your Aunt Helen are with them, and of course it's holiday, and all you gang are at home. 'Well,' I said, 'They're sensible children and I'd trust them to look after a camp, even though Marina's a tomboy, and Timothy's a wild goat. Why not turn them loose to look after themselves like Clancy and I used to do.' But your mother said——"

Mrs Harrington interrupted him. "I said I wouldn't hear of it, unless someone came to visit you every day, and unless you promised to ring up every evening from Clancy's house. Mrs Clancy says she doesn't mind just keeping an eye on you too. But you don't have to go if you don't feel like it. The thing is I thought it might be more fun for you than being around the house when I'm so very busy."

"Mum, we'd love it!" Skip cried, almost dancing with excitement. "Wouldn't we, you kids?"

The other two Harringtons shouted, "Yes! Yes! Yes!" over and over again and they actually did dance —a stamping war dance of joy around the little room.

"Careful! You'll have the place in pieces!" warned Mr Harrington, and then he joined in too, waltzing Mrs Harrington up and down.

All the children could think of now was camping out in a cabin, mossy green on the outside, blue and white on the inside, with lots of sunny days and plenty of room to shout in, and all summer seemed to stretch like a bright playground before them.

3
The Sausage Thief

Soon after this, Mr and Mrs Harrington left for home, guessing wisely that their children wanted to be left alone to get on with the serious business of camping as soon as possible. Outside the sun still shone hot on the grassy places, and the stream still called to them as it rattled over its slippery brown stones, but now the children could only think of Clancy's cabin, new and mysterious like an Aladdin's cave that might hold bright treasure. It was not just the fresh paint or the bunks, or the sheepskin rug on the floor. For the first time in all the times they had been there, the cabin was theirs—not Clancy's, not even their father's—and it was the feeling of owning that gave it this different magic.

In its own way it did turn out to be a treasure cave, though the treasures were all everyday things. In the box cupboards, and on the new sharp-edged shelves, they found all sorts of things that campers need—things that they had not had time, yet, to think of for themselves—a frying-pan, a saucepan, a wire grid for putting over their campfire, a toasting-fork with a long handle, and a billy. Behind the door in the main room were a spade and a bag of potatoes for roasting.

With a little ledge all to itself, a packet of matches sat squarely against the wall. Under it lay a note in Mr Harrington's breezy handwriting. "Bet you thought I'd forgotten these."

Timothy even discovered a large enamel basin which held a blue jug and a piece of yellow soap.

"We won't have to do dishes, will we?" he asked restlessly, wriggling his shoulders.

"We'll have to do a few, I suppose—wash ourselves too," Skip said thoughtfully. He stopped suddenly, and his eyes opened wide. "Listen! What's that?"

"What?" Timothy demanded, staring hard at his brother.

"I heard it too!" Marina said. "It sounded like someone prowling through the gorse—Daddy come back to scare us!"

But when they looked outside, the slope of grass and gorse was empty and innocent and, unless Mr Harrington was curled up small in the heart of a gorse bush, nobody was there.

"I did hear someone though!" protested Skip. "Someone running on tiptoe, and a rustling sound!"

"You're scared! Skippy's scared already!" jeered Timothy, starting a strange sideways dance just out of Skip's reach, but Marina said,

"No he isn't, Tim! I heard it too—a quick sort of running sound. There's no one here though, so I s'pose it must have been the wind. Come on! Let's look at the bunks."

"It wasn't the wind!" Skip said. "It was something else—something PROWLING!"

As they went in through the main room, Timothy stopped to stare, with a very pleased look in his eye too, at the food Mr Harrington had left for them. There were sausages to cook over the campfire, homemade wholemeal bread, butter, a small round cheese and a big plastic bag of salad—tomatoes, fresh green lettuce, radishes and a cucumber.

Best of all were an egg-and-bacon pie, and a long, rich-smelling salami sausage.

"There's enough for a year!" Marina declared, thumping Timothy in her enthusiasm, and then pushing him with a friendly knee through into the back room.

Here again, nothing had been forgotten. Skip said, rather wistfully,

"Dad must have had some fun planning all this. In a way, though, it'ud have been better if he'd let us do it all ourselves."

"Next time!" said Marina cheerfully. "There'll be lots of times." She picked up a pillow in one of the two lower bunks. "These are your pyjamas, Tim, so this'll be where you sleep."

Timothy's pleased grin was suddenly wiped from his face. "But I want the top one!" he cried.

Skip sighed. He hated fights, but Timothy, sturdy and freckled, his hair sticking up in a wiry brown crest, seemed to feel he had to make up for being the youngest, by being the fiercest as well. Often and often, Skip gave in to him, just to keep the peace, but this time he was determined not to. He wanted the top bunk too much himself. He opened his mouth to insist that it was his, feeling his cheeks grow hot with anger when, for the second time that afternoon, something mysterious happened.

From the next room came a curious thudding and clicking and rattling as something, only half glimpsed, whisked out through the open door. They scrambled out after it, but once again the gorse and brown grass had hidden the intruder. The whole summer scene was like a gold and green mask, smiling but secret. Marina felt as if eyes they could not see were watching them from everywhere.

"I didn't see what it was, did you?" Skip asked her. "Some sort of animal, I suppose, after our eats."

Timothy looked sharply at him and then ran back into the kitchen. His voice floated out, savage and sad:

"It's taken the LONG sausage—my *favourite*."

Skip sighed. "It's a pity it didn't like tomatoes," he said bitterly. "We've got plenty of those. Let's pack the food away quickly and get outside."

In the kitchen-room Timothy was standing staring into space very thoughtfully. As Skip and Marina came in, he seemed to wake up again, and he said,

"You can have the top bunk, Skippy!" in a warm generous voice.

"Well, thank you!" said Skip, surprised. "Though it was mine anyway."

Outside the sun was settling comfortably into the valley, finding out all its favourite places. The shadows in the creases of the hills grew blurred and soft, as if a giant had smudged them with his thumb. The Harrington children made a butter cooler for themselves, hollowing out a cave in the bank of the creek and lining it with stones, then, as they had done many times at home, they built a fireplace out of more stones, collected the firewood and wandered over to Clancy's house to get a jug of milk. But all the time they felt they were not alone. Someone or something was watching them from somewhere hidden, watching and waiting for them to turn their backs. It didn't spoil their afternoon, but each rustle of the wind made them look round quickly, and their ears were always listening for any different sound.

Darkness with its promise of firelight and candle-light seemed to come very slowly, and the tops of the

28

hills remained obstinately bright and sunny. Yet, at last, the time came when they lit their fire and squatted around it, staring at the first little flames that leaped so joyously into the evening air.

Skip pricked the sausages, while Marina swizzled butter around in the pan.

"Cook 'em all now!" he muttered. "Have some cold tomorrow."

Before long a rich salty sausage smell rose with the grey camp smoke and floated over the gorse.

Timothy, sitting away from the campfire to avoid the smoke, suddenly had the curious feeling that he was being watched. Marina and Skip were busy, one with the fire, the other stirring sausages with a stick, so it was nothing to do with either of them. Timothy wriggled uneasily. A rustle sounded in the gorse behind him and he turned slowly, almost as if he didn't want to look round, and stared into keen brown eyes watching him from the shadows. His heart banged like a drum in his chest, and then went galloping away as if it was trying to escape from something.

"Look!" he screamed, and his brother and sister both stared, startled, where he pointed, Marina trying to see through a fine curtain of tangled hair. The eyes belonged to a hairy ginger face, wearing a wide black mask across it. A long mouth hung open showing clean white teeth, and a lolling, hopeful, pink tongue.

"It's only a dog," Skip said. "What did you have to scare us for?"

"It's the sausage thief come back for more," declared Marina. "It's a nice old dog though."

It was no particular sort of dog, just a rough-coated, thin animal with crooked ears and friendly eyes, and a flapping tail like a gay question mark.

"I know I'm not much," it seemed to be saying, "but how about a bite, eh?"

"Just a dog!" Timothy said, still panting a little with fright. "Gee, thank goodness! I thought it was a—a—a— I dunno what I thought it was," he ended.

"Give it some sausage!" Marina said warmly. "Here's a burnt bit."

So the dog became one of the camping party and when, much later after putting the fire out and having a bit of a wash, they went to bed by candlelight, scorched by sun and fire and very happy, the dog went with them, to curl up on Timothy's bed.

"I like this dog," Timothy said drowsily. "I'm glad it was only a dog that stole our salami and not a worse sort of thing. That's why I let you have the bunk, Skip. I thought if a possum or bull or some wild thing got in at us, I could get away from a bottom bunk more quickly."

Skip looked startled and thoughtful. Then he grinned in the gloom. He couldn't help being amused at the way Timothy always took care of himself.

By candlelight the bunkroom looked as if its walls were dancing; deep dark corners seemed like gateways to mysterious lands. Thinking of Timothy and watching the flickering shadows, Skip noticed one funny curved shadow cast on the bunkroom ceiling. He put out his hand and felt along the bare beam. His searching fingers encountered something round and long that gritted against his finger nails. Someone had pushed what seemed to be a tin between the gap and the roof.

Skip thought of wriggling it out, but he was already half asleep. "I'll look at it tomorrow," he decided, letting his arm fall again.

"Hey, shall I put out the candle?" hissed Marina from below.

"O.K.," Skip murmured. "Isn't it good, camping?"

"It's terrific!" Marina replied solemnly. "G'night!" she puffed.

For a moment the shadows danced crazily over the walls. Then the little flame went out, and inky darkness rushed into the small room, with its three bunks and its tin hidden secretly under the roof beam.

4
What Skip Found

That night Skip dreamed that a long thin arm came down out of the tin under the rafter and tried to snatch his hair. He woke up with a fright and was in fact too alarmed to go to sleep again for some time. It was hardly surprising that he slept longer than the other two, and woke up to find they were already awake and gone. Neither was it surprising that Skip's first drowsy thoughts should turn to the tin under the rafter. He remembered its curious curved shadow. If it hadn't been for that shadow he would never have seen it, for it was the same rusty colour as the wood. As it was, he found it quickly, kneeling in his bunk, his hair brushing the roof. It was like Skip to hesitate for a moment before trying to pull it out, thinking it might be there to stop a leak, but at last he tugged at it, and it broke into pieces, showering his bunk with rust. This was not all. Down out of it fell a long rolled-up paper, apparently brown with age. Skip's first curiosity grew stronger as he straightened it out gingerly, feeling that it might crumble between his fingers.

It had writing on it, and a drawing—this he saw at a glance. Then, as he read the heading, his mouth fell open and he sat there looking quite foolish with surprise. In fading capital letters it read—"PATTERN FOR THE FINDING OF TREASURE".

Beneath this was the pattern itself and Skip looked at it eagerly. His heart beat wildly. "I know what this means!" he thought. Then in the next minute he wasn't so sure.

Footsteps in the kitchen made him push the paper under his pillow. Skip did not feel ready to share his discovery with Marina and Timothy, who burst in, the dog leaping at their heels, wind-blown and shining, smelling of cows and grass and gorse. Timothy's face was red and pop-eyed and he was obviously full of news and excitement.

"Gee, you're lazy!" Marina cried. "We've been up ages, over to the cowshed to see the milking. Clancy gave us three eggs, one each for breakfast."

"Guess what, Skippy," cried Timothy, and didn't even wait for Skip to reply. "Clancy says this dog can be my dog and I can keep him."

"He didn't really say that," said Marina scornfully. "He said the dog got left behind by a shearing gang, and if the man who owned him didn't come back for him soon and Daddy didn't mind, well, then Tim could have him."

Skip blinked like a dazed owl and said nothing.

"Have him to keep!" screamed Tim. "And he can stay with us while we're camping. I'm going to call him some name. I haven't thought of a good enough name yet though."

"Hey, Skip," Marina said, "do you know what I thought we could do today? Follow the creek up into the hills to where it goes underground. Clancy says he and Dad used to do that—and it would be fun. The creek's overgrown like a jungle in parts. What do you think?"

Skip nodded slowly, and then saw that Marina and Timothy were staring at him puzzled by his silence and vagueness.

"Yes, it'd be good," he made himself say. "We'll do that. We'll take something to eat too. Go and get ready—I'll be out in a minute."

Fortunately Marina and Timothy liked this idea and went tumbling out again down to the creek to get the butter, the dog bounding after them. Skip pulled out the piece of paper and began to study it again.

The pattern was a line of circles all about the same size but not equally spaced. There were three in a group, one on its own and two overlapping. Below

this was a zigzagging line and below this again a second
line that did not zigzag but which humped its back up
like a caterpillar so that, at its highest point, it cut
through the lower pointy parts of the zigzag. On this
lower, caterpillar-like line were three spots each as
big as a new penny, one on the right, one on the left
and one where the caterpillar cut through the zigzag.
This last one had been coloured red. The other two
were black. They must have been heavily inked in,
Skip thought somewhere in the back of his mind.

His first feeling that he knew what it meant, that it

was something he lived with every day faded into bewilderment. He knew that it was impossible that there should be any real treasure—pirate treasure—in this quiet farming valley, but there had to be a reason for this carefully hidden map. As he looked at it the thought came to him that it was all part of his father's joke, put there for him to find. Dad had often told them how his grandfather had made wonderful treasure hunts for him when he was a boy and how he and Clancy had ridden all over the valley seeking out clues.

"Good old Dad. I can just imagine him copying this old-fashioned writing and ironing this page with a hot iron to make it look old and brown, and searching for the old rusty tin. Dad would love doing it—it would make him grin like anything." Skip grinned too and looked at the pattern again. Once again he felt that startled feeling of recognizing it, and once again the memory was gone before he could catch it.

"Maybe the writing explains it," he thought, scrambling down from his bunk and over to the window where the light was better. Outside he could hear Marina and Timothy coming up the hill arguing about something. He read quickly and anxiously, worried least they should come in and catch him.

"Turn the world over and if you're not blind,
   The way to a treasure you're certain to find.
   North, East or West they may each play a part,
   But none has a treasure concealed in its heart.

North, East or West you pursue at your cost,
You must go by the South or be
  go by the South or be
  go by the South or be totally lost.

"It makes sense in a way," Skip thought sadly, "but it doesn't help." He considered briefly and then decided to put the map back under the rafter saying nothing to Marina and Timothy for the present.

"If I think about it I'm more likely to work it out," he told himself. Deep down he wanted to keep his secret to himself for a while before sharing it with the other two, and to enjoy the special excited feeling it gave him. He had just returned the paper to its old hiding-place when Marina and Timothy came into the kitchen, teasing him because he was still in bed, and full of plans for their expedition up the creek. Skip found it hard to be interested, for his mind was elsewhere.

Clancy's farm backed onto a long ridge of hills in the south. Beyond the hills was the city of Wellington, and beyond the city the sea. At present the hills were a light yellowish brown in colour, except for the gullies which cut deeply into their tawny sides. However hot the summer sun grew it could not tan the green out of the native bush and gorse which grew together in these gullies. Out of one such gully came the small stream that flowed down through the foot-hills and past Clancy's cabin—so that, when at last the children were going upstream, hunting eels and crawlies as they went, they were moving closer and closer to the big hills whose gentle shapes against the sky were part of their everyday world.

The stream itself turned out to be a rich, wonderful place—a winding water road whose banks were sometimes so high that the dry cocksfoot grass met in a brittle arch over the children's heads. The water was clear, not like glass, but like honey out of the comb.

As they got higher they paused by a waterfall and, looking back, saw the light-coloured January land marked with unexpected green squares which meant fields of lucerne or turnips, saw the deep summer-green of the poplars and willows and the spiky dark shapes of the firs. Then they turned on up the stream, into the deep spear-head of a gully, its stony walls covered in rangiora and native fuchsia. The breeze fluttered the wide rangiora leaves so that their silver linings flashed. Green and silver, green and silver, the rangiora semaphored a secret message to the children, but they could not read what the trees were saying.

At last the stream vanished suddenly and mysteriously into a stony patch of ground. Farther up the gully it would appear again. Why it chose to take this subterranean dive no one could tell. By now the children were tired of the cold tug of the creek at the ankles and decided to scale the gully wall—a prickly adventure—and come out onto the golden shoulder of the hill, scaring a few sheep and some shy young black bullocks as they did so.

Resting and examining their scratches they had no time at first for the new wide view that lay at their feet. Then getting their breath again they started pointing out landmarks to each other—there was Clancy's, the red roof far to the right was their own home. The blue-black serpent was the sealed road, and the little blue beetle running along it was really Mr Harland's truck. It was Marina who remarked on a strange horseshoe curve also on the left clearly seen, even though it was as if it was part of the paddocks. The two ends of the horseshoe reached down into the plain, nearly touching the road, one end about a mile from the other. The rounded top of the horseshoe cut clearly through the bushy foothills.

"Trees all along it," said Marina. "It looks like a huge ditch in a way, but it's too shallow. What is it?"

"That's the old road!" Skip said lazily. "It used to curve up around like that until they straightened it out, years ago."

"It's more like a caterpillar than a road," Timothy said with a chuckle. Skip's mouth and eyes opened wide and round for the second time that day.

He stared at the foothills and the line of the old road. Then he twisted round and frowned intently at the hill behind them. Very slowly a wide smile spread over his face.

"What are you laughing at?" asked Timothy uneasily.

Skip turned a daring somersault on the hillside. "You'll never guess until I tell you!" he said. "Something terrific!"

"What, then?" inquired Marina, baffled.

"Wait and see!" Skip replied smugly, enjoying his secret.

5
Rain on the Roof

They had lunch on the warm shoulder of the hill before setting off back to Clancy's cabin. Funnily enough, the dog who had the least to eat seemed the happiest of all when they finally made their way downstream again. His tail wagged constantly as he weaved through the grass and bushes on the bank, and his open mouth seemed to grin down at the children.

There were several reasons why Skip, Marina and Timothy did not enjoy going down the stream as much as they had enjoyed coming up it. To begin with they were now scratched, damp and therefore uncomfortable. Secondly, Timothy and Marina were cross with Skip for being so mysterious, and walked together behind him, leaving him on his own. However, for once Skip did not mind. He felt his secret knowledge, warm and exciting inside him, and every now and then he turned round to look back at the hills.

"I'm sure I'm right!" he thought each time. Then he would say the names of the hills over to himself. "The Princesses, yes, Singleton's Hill—the Chopping Block!" and he would feel even happier.

The only thing that worried him was the sight of clouds creeping up behind the hills. At first they were white and fluffy, but they rapidly became grey and dirty coloured and spread over the sky swallowing the sun.

"I hope it's not going to rain," muttered Skip. "That would spoil everything . . . rain would. We'd probably have to go home."

With the sunshine gone, the wind seemed to become sharp and cold, cutting against them unpleasantly. It was no wonder that Marina's voice was disagreeable when they came home at last to Clancy's cabin.

"All right then—where's your old secret?" she snapped at Skip.

Without a word he went into the bunkroom and rescued the paper from its hiding-place under the rafter.

"It's something Dad must've left for us to find," he said. "He's arranged a treasure hunt for us."

"Did he tell you?" asked Timothy excitedly.

"No . . . I found it this morning where he'd hidden it," Skip replied.

Timothy glared at him. "Why didn't you tell us?" he cried. "Gee, you're mean, Skip, a mean secret-keeper."

Skip felt suddenly apologetic. "I didn't understand it," he explained humbly. "Not at first!"

Marina was holding one end of the paper down and frowning at it. "Hey, but this is *old*," she said slowly. "It's all brown and the writing's all old-fashioned."

Skip instantly explained that their father could have faked both the colour and the writing to make the paper look really old, and added that it was just the sort of thing he would enjoy doing.

Marina agreed. "The details!" she exclaimed triumphantly. "Dad loves to get details right—like remembering to put our pyjamas under our bunk pillows." She looked at the pattern again. "I can't understand it at all," she said helplessly.

Timothy cried, "I can't read that old writing! Read it to me!" So Marina read the rhyme over to him.

There was a silence.

"Well, I don't know!" Timothy said. "It's just mad. I've never heard of a *pattern* for finding treasure. Anyway what's it got to do with the rhyme? 'Turn the world over . . .!' What's it *mean*?"

"I think it means search through the world," said Skip doubtfully.

"I don't really see where the rhyme fits in at all. I know what the pattern means though. It's a sort of map all the time."

"What does it mean?" asked Marina sharply.

"Mr Know-Everything!" added Timothy.

This was Skip's great moment. He took a deep breath.

"When I saw the pattern it reminded me of something, but I couldn't think what it was. Then when we were up on the hill, I saw that the old road curved up like the loopy line in the pattern. Suddenly I just *knew* what the circles reminded me of. Don't you see? It's the hills—our own hills. Three circles in a group—that's the Princesses (you know—three Princesses like in the fairy stories). One on its own—that's Singleton's Hill—and the two circles overlapping mean the Chopping Block—you know how it looks like two hills melted into one but still with separate peaks, or as if someone had split its top into two with an axe." Skip stopped and looked at the others anxiously.

"I suppose," said Marina, "that the zigzag line means the foothills. But what about the three places marked on the curving line—on the old road?"

"Well," said Skip eagerly, "I think that the right-hand one is Clancy's house, and I think the left-hand one must be ours. But the one where the old road crosses the foothills is coloured red. That must be where the treasure is, and tomorrow we must go and look for it. We'll go along the road until we come to the place where the old road branches off (I know where that is, I think), then we'll go along that old road and see what we shall see. It's over Mr Harland's land but he won't mind. I expect the treasure place is pretty obvious once you know where to look." He looked at the pattern lovingly, and then an expression of disappointment crept over his face. "There's only one thing . . . I'm sure these circles stand for the hills, but they're at the top of the pattern which means the *north*, doesn't it, and our hills are in the south. It says in the rhyme to go by the south or be totally lost!"

"It's not a real map," Timothy pointed out. "It's just a *pattern*."

Marina looked at them, and then asked cautiously,

"It does say to go by the south—says it three times. Skip, suppose you turn the map upside-down? Would the circles be in the south then? Would that make it right?"

Skip stared down at the paper and then grinned all over his face.

"Gosh!" he said. "You've solved it. That's what the rhyme says to do, doesn't it? 'Turn the world over and if you're not blind, the way to a treasure you're certain to find.' I didn't even think of it like that."

Skip and Marina beamed at one another feeling full of cleverness, but Timothy just felt sour and left out. He had made no grand discoveries. Only the nameless dog, pressing its nose against his hand seemed his friend.

"Imagine Dad's face when he hears we've solved

it already!" Marina said happily, and Timothy had an idea of his own.

"Don't let's tell him," he said anxiously. "Don't let's say anything about it—not even let on we've found the map. He'll get all impatient waiting for us to find it, and then we'll come out with the treasure and surprise him—it'll be a joke on Dad."

Feeling generous towards Timothy, Marina and Skip agreed promptly, even thinking to themselves that it was a fine idea to have a joke on Mr Harrington, so all three children felt well pleased with themselves and with each other.

Late that afternoon when they were swimming in the creek, splashing each other (and the barking dog too), their father and mother came to visit them. Mrs Harrington looked worried when she saw them swimming because it had grown so cold and cloudy, but Mr Harrington laughed and said they were a tough lot. The children dressed hastily, and put on the jerseys their parents had brought them. Then they had a grand tour of the camp. Mr and Mrs Harrington enjoyed it all thoroughly, and were full of praise and admiration for the butter cooler in the creek bank, for the fireplace and for the steamy oven of hot stones, embers and turf where potatoes were slowly cooking, Maori fashion, for tea that night. Mostly, however, they admired the dog.

"He's a dog with a laugh in his eye," Mr Harrington remarked. "What do you call him?"

Timothy suddenly said, "Treasure! That's his name!"

Marina and Skip glared at him so that he turned red, but Mr Harrington didn't even look twinkly.

"It's a grand name!" he said. "If nobody wants him, and you're very good, we'll see if we can't talk your mother into letting us have him."

"Maybe!" said Mrs Harrington carefully.

Timothy let out a howl of joy. Skip and Marina grinned with pleasure. They waved goodbye to their parents, feeling that they were the most generous parents in the world. Then the thought of treasure—not dog Treasure, but the other sort—filled their minds once more and, as evening came on, as they ate their baked potatoes and slices of egg-and-bacon pie, they talked about the treasure—*what* it could be, *where* it could be hidden, until they were almost too excited to sleep. At last they did go to sleep, but it was not for very long.

Skip woke with a start somewhere in the dark part of the morning to find rain trickling onto his face through a leak in the roof. Half scrambling, half falling, he reached the floor bringing his blankets with him. Treasure woke up and began barking wildly, then seized a blanket and worried it, growling. Marina and Timothy struggled awake out of dreams of gold and jewels. The rain was pelting down, drumming, dull and steady, on the roof of Clancy's cabin. Fumbling and dropping matches Marina lit the candle and they blinked at one another.

"It's raining!" Skip said blankly. "Pouring with rain! It's leaking onto my bed and I'll have to sleep in the kitchen."

"We'd all better!" Marina said. "Or we'll all get a bit damp. We'll make an explorer's bed. Come on, Tim."

Timothy stood quite still, blinking, then he gave a cry of protest and despair.

"It mustn't rain!" he shouted. "We're going treasure-hunting tomorrow! It mustn't rain!"

This was exactly what Skip was feeling himself, but he felt also that as he was the oldest he must set a good example.

"It'll probably clear up, Tim," he said. "Don't get miserable yet. There's nothing we can do, anyhow."

"Clear up!" Timothy exclaimed, staring at him as if he had suggested they fly around the room to keep warm. "Clear up! Listen to it. More likely there'll be a flood."

The rain boomed down sounding like the guns of an army besieging Clancy's cabin, as the dejected campers began to make a bed for themselves on the kitchen floor.

6
The Road to the Treasure

It seemed a long restless time until morning looked in at the little window and, though it was a grey restless morning, it was no longer cold. Some time in the night the wind had turned to the north and was blowing in great strong wailing gusts around Clancy's cabin, but the rain had stopped, and in between the shifting clouds, seeming very high above them, the children could see pale blue sky and watery sunshine.

They had a visitor almost before they were awake. . . . Treasure the dog began to flop his tail uncertainly on the floor, and the next minute Clancy came in in his oilskins inviting them to breakfast over at the farmhouse.

There was no doubt that it was very pleasant to sit in Mrs Clancy's clean scrubbed kitchen eating eggs and bacon and drinking cocoa, and it was not long before the uncomfortable night, with all its tossings and turnings, its quarrelling over blankets, and its uneasy sleep, seemed adventurous and quite funny. Skip rang his parents and assured them that all was well, then they thanked Mrs Clancy warmly for their breakfast, and went out into the windy wild morning. The sun was struggling with the flying clouds which were trying to cover him over again, but there was a lot of blue sky and the north was clear.

The rainy night had done its damage, however. Skip's bunk was soaked, Marina's, beneath his, was damp, and worst of all the creek had risen sufficiently to wash the milk and butter out of their butter cooler and to fill it with sticks and mud. The blue milk jug was gone.

However, as Skip said, there was no use worrying about spilt milk or even milk that has been carried off by a flood. They forgot these irritating troubles, packed the remains of the egg-and-bacon pie, tomatoes and plums, and set off over Clancy's paddocks, while Treasure, pleased to be going for a walk, ran ahead of them shaking the rain drops from the grass.

So after all they were going treasure hunting, and while the children watched the live hairy Treasure nosing the grass and exploring in circles around them, in their mind's eye a different treasure shone. What could it be? Each of them wondered. What could be hidden at the place marked in red on the map?

Skip carried the map proudly, feeling like the leader of the expedition. He felt at last that he was doing something truly adventurous that no one could blame him for. So many of the truly adventurous things seemed to be things that boys shouldn't do.

The grass was brown, but underneath it they could see the new blades coming up, green and hopeful.

"The hills and the grass must be glad of the rain," Marina said, leaning into the wind, feeling it tug and twist in her hair.

They climbed over a fence and came into the road, Treasure squeezing his long rough body under it. His tongue hung joyously out like a pink flag waving at the world. Skip was filled with thoughts of his map and Timothy was thinking what his share in the treasure might be, but Marina looked around her as they went and let everything she saw fill her mind. She saw the sparkle of rain drops on the fir trees as they walked under them, and turned her face up so that she could see the blue sky through dark branches. Late foxgloves, short-stemmed but still brave, bent out from the tangled cocksfoot grass and gorse, and big purple clovers mixed with little creamy ones in patches all along the road.

"Somehow, after the rain," Marina thought, "the air seems special—all fresh and good, and everything enjoys being alive." She smiled at Treasure who seemed to grin back, flattening his ears with pleasure as she patted his sleek flat-boned head. They walked and walked.

"Next bend!" Skip said cheerfully.

The next bend revealed another long stretch of road.

"Next bend!" said Skip anxiously. "Maybe we've missed it," he muttered.

The road was empty of traffic. Once a truck rattled by them and dogs on the back barked at Treasure who tore madly after it and returned with his ears flicked inside-out. Once a car went by with someone in it who waved out to them, but they could not see who it was.

Then at last they came to the place—or Skip said it was the place.

"Somewhere over that bank! See that break in the top of it. There used to be a little sort of hill here and they cut half of it away when they made this road. The old road used to go over it."

Parked on the side of the road close against the bank was a rattly looking green car.

"Look at the bomb!" jeered Timothy. "Look at the old jalopy bomb!"

Sure enough, when they had climbed the bank they found Skip was right. A long way stretched before them. It was no different from the paddocks around in its grassiness or its colour, but it dipped down into the ground and was fringed with trees and bushes.

"It's Mr Harland's land now. He runs sheep on it," Skip said. "Dad says it's not very good land around here. Not long now and we'll be there."

"You keep on saying that," objected Timothy, "and gosh, I'm hungry. What do you think the treasure will be?"

"Books!" Marina said.

"Just because you like books," Timothy cried, "you think everyone's got to like them! I think it might be an electric train set for us."

"Don't be silly!" was all Skip said.

"Or a clockwork one!" muttered Timothy, crushed but defiant.

There was something enchanting about the green road leading over the fields deeper into some mysterious land where magical people lived. Marina thought that there might be unicorns, but all they met was four sheep wearing short January coats who started and fled on short thin legs. The road dipped and rose as they got into the hills. In places it still had banks, gentle and dark with ferns and mosses.

Very nearly they missed what they had come so far to find.

"Hey, look!" Timothy said nervously. "Treasure's found a gate."

"Don't be mad!" answered Skip impatiently, for he was tired. Then he saw Timothy was right. Treasure was nosing a gate hanging by one hinge from an old gatepost, almost entirely hidden by elderberry trees and tall grass. The wide umbrellas of the elderberry flowers seemed to be trying to conceal what lay beyond, but Marina said,

"Bricks in the ground! It's a path to somewhere. Let's have a look, Skip."

Skip wrinkled his forehead uncertainly. "Maybe we should ask?" he replied.

Marina laughed. "Ask who? The trees?" she said, and pushed the gate aside. It swung sadly under her hand. "Let's go in!"

Followed by Timothy and the dog Treasure she set off down the path, and vanished under a tree with long drooping branches covered in flowers like orange trumpets—datura trees Skip thought they were called. He had to follow, of course. Grass grew long between the bricks.

Beyond the datura trees were hydrangea bushes gone wild, taller than he was. He had to push his way through them. As he did so he heard Marina exclaim in surprise somewhere ahead. Through at last, he too cried out astonished. They had found an old house, hidden in trees from the road, the fields and probably from the hills as well.

It was a very old house, falling slowly to pieces as the rain, the wind, the sun all beat in turn upon its walls. At one end the veranda had fallen in. Yet it was still lovely in its own green way, for wistaria had covered some of its scars and pink rose climbed luxuriantly up the wall and even over the roof, which was green with age and moss. The children wandered around, too surprised and scared to say much. Timothy thought of home, which was so ordinary and un-mysterious, and he felt very glad Treasure was with them. Marina remembered stories of people who had wandered into strange lands and had come out to find five hundred years gone by. She was a little afraid, and yet at the same time she felt she loved this lost house alone and dying here in its own secret place.

"Someone has pruned the fruit trees," Skip said gloomily. "Look!" He pointed to faded leafy pieces lying under a plum tree. "Those have been clipped off. Someone lives here. We'd better go."

"Listen!" Marina said, and they listened. A deep silence rushed in on them. Somewhere a sheep bleated and Treasure rustled through the grass, but there was nothing human . . . only wind and animal sounds.

"No one's here," said Marina. "Let's try the door and go inside."

"No!" said Timothy. "This is a witch place, and I'm scared."

"Silly!" Skip replied. "We'd better not though, Marina. It is someone's place, and it is scary."

"It isn't scary!" Marina objected, climbing onto the veranda. "But it's awfully sad to think of this old house going to pieces here all on its own. Look, the door isn't locked." She went a few steps into the hall. It seemed long and high and gloomy, and on her right was a door a little bit open. She pushed it and it creaked stiffly as it opened a few more inches.

"Look out!" cried Skip in alarm, "The whole place might come down on you!"

At this point Timothy screamed. "Someone's here! I heard someone walking . . . just like when Treasure stole the sausage."

Marina was scornful. "No one's here!" she said angrily. "It's just an old empty house."

She opened the door on her right and looked into the room beyond, ignoring her hesitating brothers. It was a kitchen, or had been in earlier days. There were the benches, the cupboards, the old wood stove set in a brick-lined recess in the wall. Everything was cobwebby, dusty, rusty, falling into decay, except for one thing. The end of the kitchen table was clean— not just dusted, but looking as if it has been scrubbed and sitting on this pale patch of wood were a tea-cup and a dainty plate with a fresh-looking sandwich on it. Marina stared at these things for a long moment—

at first nervously, then thoughtfully. At last she closed the door and turned back to her brothers.

"It's all quiet and dusty and empty," she declared firmly. "No one's here but us. Don't be cowards. Come in and look around a bit. I'm sure the treasure will be here somewhere."

7
The Strange Old Woman

When Marina told them the house looked quite empty
the boys ventured up the steps and into the hall. They
stared nervously at the wallpaper hanging in loops and
trails as it peeled off the walls, and sniffed the strange
smell of dust, decay and cobwebs—the *old* smell of a
neglected house. Marina was opening a door, half way
along the hall, opposite a stair which led up into the
darkness of the upper storey.

"Here's the sitting-room!" Marina said. "Look!"
Her voice sounded unexpectedly loud in the musty
stillness. Skip whispered,

"What a spooky sort of place—a funny spooky

place." His whisper ran around the high ceiling with its own soft quick echo chasing after it.

"It smells a bit like the bush!" Timothy said. "Like wet dead leaves!"

At the other end of the hall was a door with panes of red-and-green glass, and the light coming through it flung patches of bright colour at their feet. Timothy stared at it with admiration as they went into the sitting-room.

It was a big room and its windows were almost entirely overgrown by creepers on the outside wall, so that it was dim, even at midday, and filled with a soft green light. It wasn't empty like the hall either. There was a huge chair with the upholstery torn, and the stuffing bulging out, an old picture in a dirty frame, and from one side of the windows a long curtain that had once been blue but was now a yellowish, whitish colour, hung in thin sad folds. The children looked at these things in silence. Then Timothy saw something else. Behind the door was a big globe as tall as his shoulder, held in a frame that was bolted to the floor. He could still see the faded outlines of countries on its peeling surface. He stared at it, quite overawed by its bigness, and wondered if it had, perhaps, belonged to a giant. This was not an idea he liked and he quickly thought that everything else was ordinary-sized, and felt better.

"Come on," Marina said, "let's go and look somewhere else. But in every other room along the hall it was the same fading, falling, dust, dirt and sadness. They wandered back again towards the stair.

"It's not so much like being in a house as like being in a hollow tree," said Marina. "If only people's things weren't here. That's what makes it sad—being reminded that people lived here. If it wasn't for that it would be just as if this house had stopped belonging to humans and had started to be like trees and plants and birds."

"A house is just a house—not a tree or a bird," said Timothy. "Shall we go upstairs?"

"Borer [type of woodworm] everywhere!" Skip said. "Better not! You might go through."

Marina immediately ran up about six stairs, turning

round to pull a face at Skip. Because of this, suddenly, without warning, a most frightening thing happened.

A voice spoke from the other end of the hall, and said,

"I wouldn't go up there, little girl. It isn't safe."

It was a light, thin voice—the sort of voice you might expect a brown autumn leaf to have—and not at all angry, but Marina overbalanced with fright and had to clutch at the stair rail. Timothy and Skip felt the hair creep on their heads, and their hearts start drumming. They all thought for one frightening moment that it was a ghost speaking and were almost too terrified to turn round. Yet, when they did so there was certainly no ghost . . . only a strange old woman who had come quietly into the hall, and was standing watching them smiling faintly.

She looked such a *small* old woman under her great round sun hat, with her thin ankles disappearing into clumpy shoes. Her smallness, the green dress she wore, the rose in the ribbon of her hat, all made her look like a funny sort of fairy creature come out of the garden. In one hand she had a Maori kitbag and in the other a pair of clippers. She had obviously just been pruning the trees and gathering some flowers. Her kitbag was overflowing with sprays of pink roses.

Treasure the dog, who had been sniffing round the hall, was just as startled as the children and burst out barking, sounding like a warship firing off its guns.

"Silly fellow!" the old woman said. "I wouldn't

64

hurt you." Her thin voice had such a warm friendly sound that Treasure's tail began to wag. He stopped barking and gave her a dog's grin instead.

Marina said, half whispering, "Do you live here?"

The old woman looked up, with a wide smile creasing her face into a net of wrinkles.

"Not now!" she answered. "I used to once. It is a long story and it was a long time ago. I'm sorry if I frightened you, but you know you frightened me too. I thought you were the ghost of someone I knew once."

"I'm sorry!" Skip said humbly.

The old woman smiled again and went on, "There I was, weeding round Dora (Dora is a plum tree I planted years ago—all my trees had names), and I heard your voices. I felt so shy of being found that I climbed into Dora's branches, and the kind old tree put her leaves round me and hid me so safely. I could just see out and when the big boy walked past I nearly fell out on top of you I got such a shock." She looked at Skip. "You are just like a boy who used to visit me years ago. His name was Esmond Harrington."

All three children cried out in astonishment.

"That *is* my name!" Skip yelled, and she nodded happily.

"Yes, I thought I couldn't be wrong, though the Esmond I knew would be grown up by now."

"It must have been our Dad!" Skip declared. "His name is Esmond too."

The dog Treasure wandered over to have a closer

look at the old woman. She patted his head. The children drew closer, feeling more certain of themselves. An old woman who had known their father wouldn't be angry with them, they were sure. She gave her wide smile at them, as if she read their thoughts.

"You don't have to be frightened of me," she said. "I have no more right to be here than you have. Let's go out on the steps and eat plums, and if I tell you why I'm here, you might tell me what you are doing here in exchange."

It was pleasant on the veranda looking into the green tangle of the old garden, free of the musty smell of the house. As their new acquaintance handed round the plums, Skip and Timothy between them told her how their father had bought back his old home, and how they all lived there now.

"That's a good thing," she said. "I was so fond of your father. He knew the names of all the trees and flowers in my garden, and he used to ask after them . . . 'How's Dora?' he would say, 'How's Henry?' as if they were friends of his too. And his grandfather— your great-grandfather that would be—was a remarkable man, such a traveller, and a friend of my husband's too. I'm glad someone lives in the Harrington house again. It's sad to see an old house fall to pieces." She looked across at the fallen-in corner of the veranda.

"Why don't you live here still?" asked Timothy boldly.

She sighed and cocked her head on one side like a

bird. "I couldn't afford to when my husband died," she answered. "He was killed in an accident, and your great-grandfather was killed with him—all a long time ago. A farmer—Mr Harland—bought the land and added it to his farm, but he had a house already and didn't want this one. And the road got changed about that time, and my poor old house got left out here all alone. No one wanted it but me. I was in Auckland for some years with my daughter Anne. When I came back I just had to come and see how my old garden was getting on. I drove out in my little car, struggled up the bank—a proper old monkey woman I must have looked too—and came along the old road. Goodness, I was surprised to see how many of my plants and trees were still struggling on their own. Dora—the plum tree, you know—had grown large—very large. There are still crocuses growing between her roots in the spring and autumn, dear little cups of gold. I came back then, and I have kept on coming back every week-end. I prune a bit here and weed a bit there, so the flowers and plants can breathe. I steal a few roses too, and some plums and parsley and mint. I don't think the farmer would mind."

"He wouldn't at all. He's nice," Marina declared. "Isn't it a long walk though?"

"It is, but you know I'm a tough old woman," was the answer. "Tough as nails or an old apple tree. I like to think of myself as an old apple tree, standing through many storms, and still enjoying the spring time." She looked up into the sky and then down at her gentle brown hands streaked with soil and the green sap of plants. Then in a brisker tone she said,

"Now, tell me why you are here."

The children looked at each other.

"Well . . ." began Skip.

"We came looking for treasure," Marina said. "Skip —show her the map."

"Treasure!" the old woman cried, so sharply that the dog Treasure began to thump with his tail. "Your father was always having treasure hunts. Let me see your map."

Skip opened it up and passed it over to her. From a pocket she took a large pair of spectacles and studied it closely. Her huge straw sun hat cast a shadow on it for a moment and then she looked up and gave, not a smile, but a real grin.

"How very fortunate that you met me," she said. "I may be able to help you with this more than you realize."

"Do you mean that you know where the treasure is?" Timothy asked.

"Not only that," this old woman answered, "but I am the one you were sent to find, believe it or not. Let me show you where it says so." And she read from the rhyme, "'You must go by the South or be totally lost'. That's the clue! 'South or be . . .'" she repeated firmly. "You see my name is Mrs Southerby and it is my name that is worked into the rhyme."

8
Timothy Turns the World Over

There was silence for a moment on the sunny veranda.

"'You must go by the South or be totally lost'," read Marina slowly. "We thought it meant to go in a southerly direction. That's partly why we came here. We didn't even know you then."

"Your great-grandfather was very fond of a joke," Mrs Southerby said. "He was always putting two meanings in the same sentence. He meant when he wrote this, 'You must go in a southerly direction and visit Mrs Southerby'. But he put it all in one line. It's like a pun . . . a play on words. How remarkable that we should have met though!"

"But," said Skip politely, frowning and puzzled, "our great-grandfather didn't write this map. Our father did . . ." His voice trailed off uncertainly. "I think," he added. After all, he was not at all sure. He thought of the rusty tin tucked under the rafters in Clancy's cabin.

Mrs Southerby's brown eyes crinkled thoughtfully. "Now, I know you're wrong about that," she said. "For I saw your great-grandfather—Old Esmond as we used to call him to distinguish him from your father who was Young Esmond in those days—I saw Old Esmond write this down and draw the pattern. He rode round to our place just two days before he was killed, and hid the treasure and wrote the clues. This was the last one and he was going to hide it in that little hut your father and Clancy O'Regan used to play in."

"We found it in Clancy's cabin," Skip said. "I thought Dad had hidden it."

"Did you ask him?" Mrs Southerby said.

"Well, no, we thought we'd pretend we hadn't found it—just as a joke—and then surprise him," Skip stammered.

"My dear Harringtons," said Mrs Southerby, "I think that it must have been there since Old Esmond your great-grandfather hid it. He was always making treasure hunts for the boys, but this was a special birthday one. Then, as I said, Old Esmond and my husband Tom were killed, just the day before your father's birthday. It was a terrible time. I suppose the treasure hunt was quite lost and forgotten. I certainly forgot it. Your father can't have found that clue you have there, and he certainly never found the treasure, for I saw it only a week ago."

"Is it safe?" cried Timothy.

"Quite safe," she answered cheerfully, "but it wasn't mine and I didn't know quite what to do with it, so I left it there."

Marina leaped up, eyes shining. "So it's really old!" she exclaimed. "And this clue has been in Clancy's cabin for years and years waiting for someone to find it, and *we* found it. It's much better than if Daddy had made a treasure hunt for us. This is *true*."

Skip too was thrilled. "We'll find it and give it to Dad!" he declared. "A birthday present about twenty years too late."

Timothy seized the dog Treasure by his forepaws and tried to dance with him.

"It will be pleasant to see one more treasure hunt in the old house," Mrs Southerby said. "I enjoy life of course, and I love driving my little old car, though I'm afraid I'm not a very reliable driver, but I'm afraid I'm a little selfish and I like to have as much of good past times, as well as good present ones, as ever I possibly can. That's why I'm always coming back to this garden. So you go and look for the treasure and I won't help you one bit . . . though I'm sure you're too clever to need any help. I'll just watch. Now off you go. I'll tell you this much. It's in a downstairs room."

There were six rooms downstairs—a kitchen, a bathroom, a sitting-room, a dining-room, a study, with a big desk still in it, and a square room, with a lot of boxes in it, facing onto the northern veranda.

"The bedrooms were all upstairs," Mrs Southerby recalled. "We liked the view over the valley."

She looked more like some good garden witch than ever, thought Marina, and wondered what would have happened if Mrs Southerby had fallen out of her plum-tree hiding-place just as they were passing. She imagined a little brown woman in a huge sun hat, clumpy shoes and a green dress tumbling out of the leaves. "It would have been like dreaming, or like *Alice in Wonderland*," she thought, and nearly giggled.

Skip, in rather a lordly fashion, still feeling he was the leader of the expedition, chose the square front room to search. The boxes and the carving on the walls around the fireplace caught his eye. In his secret mind Skip thought he might well discover a hidden panel or cupboard. Marina had much the same thoughts when she chose the study to explore. She felt that the old desk, with all its drawers and pigeon-holes might easily be the hiding-place.

"It was so big I didn't have room for it when I moved," said Mrs Southerby. "I always meant to collect the things I left because no new owner would want them. But there was no new owner."

73

Timothy found himself left with a choice of the bathroom, kitchen, sitting-room and dining-room, which was not so much as it sounds. All except the sitting-room were quite bare. He felt that the others had the best places and his forehead grew knotted with frowns.

"It's not fair," he muttered. Treasure the dog nosed his hand trying to be comforting.

"Oh well!" sighed Timothy, and went off to look in the bathroom.

Mrs Southerby went from room to room, watching them as they searched.

In the square room Skip struggled with boxes. He worked carefully, looking in each one and then stacking it against a wall. As the boxes were disturbed spiders, some of them quite large, scuttled away on long active legs. Skip wasn't afraid of spiders, but they still startled him when he came across them—they were so dark and scrambling. Dust rose in the air about him and danced in a sunbeam.

Marina searched the old desk, hoping for a secret drawer. It was quite empty, but she decided to go through it again, pulling the drawers right out this time. Mrs Southerby came in for a moment.

"Poor old desk! But I really don't have room for it in the little cottage I live in now."

"Could you sell it?" Marina asked shyly.

Mrs Southerby looked thoughtfully at the desk.

"Do you know," she said at last, "I'd almost rather

think of it falling to pieces with the house now. It's sad, of course, but it's peaceful and dignified in a funny way. Now, I must go and see how Timothy is getting on."

Nothing could have been barer or less interesting than the bathroom, though the bath still stood there on its small iron feet, empty inside and all around. The kitchen had cupboards, but Timothy could find nothing in them—not even a jam jar or a knife or a duster cloth. Shuffling into the sitting-room he looked around him crossly—at the big old chair, the faded curtain, the globe bolted to the floor. None of these things suggested treasure to him at all. Yet, as he looked around something came into his mind like the echo of a song. Timothy felt it was important in some way. He tried to pin it down, just as Skip had yesterday tried to remember what the circles of the pattern reminded him of. Timothy looked around the room again, and once more the song came into his mind and went before he could take hold of it. Was it a song? Or a poem? He struggled with his memory. Once more his eyes flickered over the room—chair, curtain, leaves at the windows—and suddenly, clear as a bell as if a voice spoke in his mind, he found what he had been searching for.

"Turn the world over and if you're not blind,
    The way to a treasure you're certain to find."

"'Turn the world over!'" Timothy exclaimed aloud

as he walked over to the globe. His heart was beating hard. "I'm sure this is it."

The big globe, the countries of the world peeling from its surface, moved slowly as Timothy tugged it round. It needed oiling. But as it turned over it thudded dully. There was something inside it. Then Timothy saw on the line of the equator, where the two halves of the globe came together, a little sticking out piece like the catch on a camera. He pressed against it and it did not stir. Timothy sighed and shook his hand, for it hurt his thumb. From behind him Mrs Southerby's gentle, light voice said,

"Try again, Timothy. Remember it's old and stiff. Try again."

There she was standing behind him smiling—well, not so much smiling as grinning in a very adventurous fashion. So Timothy tried again. He pressed the catch and pressed it again and suddenly it moved, slowly at first, and then all at once. The globe sprang in half at the equator and Timothy saw at a glance that the bottom half of it was filled with dusty parcels. A moment later Skip, still shifting spidery boxes, Marina still searching for secret drawers in the old desk, heard Timothy screaming excitedly.

"Come on, you kids! I've found it! I've found it! It's the treasure and I've found it!"

9
The Treasure

The other children came running to see what Timothy had found. Excited by the shouting, Treasure the dog began to bark wildly, wagging his tail. Mrs Southerby grinned, looking more and more like a mischievous old witch-woman. The globe of the world stood open like a round box, and none of them doubted, looking at the parcels it held, that this was the treasure that Big Esmond had hidden for their father, Little Esmond, all those years ago.

"How did you find it?" asked Skip, too excited to be jealous of the prancing Timothy.

"I just looked around," Timothy replied, "and I remembered Mrs Southerby had said that our great-grandfather liked to put two meanings in one lot of words. I thought when he said 'Turn the world over . . .' in the rhyme he might have meant *this* world, this globe of the world, and not just turning the map upside-down." Timothy looked full of pride and pleasure and did a funny little shuffling dance of triumph as he spoke. "So I turned it over and saw the catch here . . . and I pressed on it, and—and——"

"Let's open them!" Skip cried. "Let's see what the treasure is."

"One at a time," said Marina quickly. "Timothy first, because he found it!"

Then Timothy did a grand thing.

"No," he said, "Skippy first, because he's the one who found the map and worked it out. He should open the first parcel."

Skip gasped a little with delight as he picked out the first brown dusty parcel.

"He's taken the BIGGEST!" Timothy muttered to Marina. "That's not manners."

It was a parcel about a foot long and round like a bottle. Indeed, it was a bottle but such a one as the children had never seen before. It was a clear, light green, like a very shallow water; and quite small, inside it, someone long ago had set a little ship sailing. It was a clipper ship, three-masted, with all its sails open and cut so that they seemed to be billowing in an enchanted silent wind. The tiny ropes seemed alive and straining against the sway and surge of the sea.

Only the flags and pennants, blue, crimson and green, hung limp at the mastheads instead of fluttering gaily. The name *Lightning* was painted on the side in gold. All three children and the old woman cried out in delight.

"I had forgotten how lovely it was," Mrs Southerby said. "Isn't it beautiful? There really was a clipper called *Lightning* in about 1860. It used to go from England to Australia. The man who made this for Old Esmond (who was only a little boy then) had once been a sailor on her."

They could have stared at it for a long time, for there was so much to see in it, but the other parcels were waiting to be opened—three other parcels—and all had been waiting for such a long time.

Marina's hand hovered over one. Mrs Southerby said quickly,

"Not that one! I've just remembered something remarkable. Marina, take the little one—the smallest."

"What! This very little one?" Marina asked, slightly dismayed.

When Mrs Southerby nodded, Marina took the tiny parcel and opened it. It held a small black box, which seemed at first to be filled with yellow silk. Carefully Marina felt in between the soft folds and found something hard and round. It was the picture of a young woman with soft brown hair and blue eyes. She wore a white flower in her blue dress, and smiled gently out at them. Marina frowned, puzzled, and turned it over.

On the back someone had written her own name. "Marina Harrington 1895".

"Who is it?" Marina cried. "Not me! And it's not Daddy's sister, Aunt Marina, because her name's Mrs Adams, and anyhow, she's fattish with glasses."

"Can't you guess?" Mrs Southerby said. "It's Old Esmond's wife, your great-grandmother. You see, Skip isn't the only one to have a family name. It seemed to me a funny present for Old Esmond to give to your father—but there you are—he said he liked giving presents that meant something, and he seemed to think your father would treasure it. It is painted on ivory, you see. Wasn't she pretty?"

Marina could scarcely tear her eyes from the face of the painted, long ago dead Marina.

"She was beautiful!" she breathed, feeling in a startled way that she was going to cry a little bit.

"Not like you!" Timothy said rudely and impatiently, grabbing the next parcel. This turned out to be a dagger in a leather sheath. It had a curved blade and a carved bronze hilt and, in spite of its years, it looked very sharp and wicked. Timothy was delighted.

"Your great-grandfather got it when travelling in China, I believe," Mrs Southerby remarked. "It was given to him by a real Chinese pirate. I understand it is not very well *balanced*, but it looks quite well balanced enough to do a lot of damage with." Mrs Southerby looked up at the ceiling. "I remember Big Esmond sitting here wrapping up these things and telling us

80

about them as he went along—I remember it more clearly than the picture I saw last week. That's because I'm old, I suppose. Old people sometimes remember back to front. That square parcel was for Clancy. Your father and Clancy were always together."

It turned out to be a big copy of *Treasure Island*, beautifully illustrated and bound in leather.

Now the globe was empty. The treasure lay before them—treasure hidden for so many years now seen again in the green light of Mrs Southerby's old sitting-room. They all stared at it . . . at the ship in the bottle, the picture, the dagger and the book.

"Daddy will be surprised!" said Skip. "They're very late birthday presents."

"Maybe he won't want them," Timothy remarked hopefully, his fingers curling round the hilt of the dagger. Skip looked at him sternly, all the more sternly because he wanted the ship in the bottle so much himself.

"We must still give them to him," he said. "They were meant for him, weren't they, Mrs Southerby?"

"They were indeed," she answered. "I'd love to see his face when he gets them."

Marina's own face suddenly lit up. "Well, why not!" she cried. "I was thinking yesterday how nice it would be to give a party for Mummy and Daddy and the Clancys—a campfire party with chops and baked potatoes and those sort of things. Why don't we? Mrs Southerby could come in her car and surprise them, we'd have tea, and then after tea we'd dive into Clancy's cabin and bring out the treasure."

Clear in her mind shone a little picture of firelight flickering on her father's face as he unwrapped his presents.

"Gee!" said Skip thoughtfully.

Mrs Southerby sat still and looked at her brown hands.

"Dad 'ud love to see you," begged Timothy. "Come on!"

She looked up at them almost shyly. "Do you really think he'd be pleased?"

"Of course he would!" exclaimed Marina. "He'd love it. He's always talking about the old days with Clancy. He'd love to meet you again like *anything*."

Mrs Southerby stood up unexpectedly. "All right,"

she said. "I'll come. I'll write my phone number down and you can ring and tell me when to come. I shall look forward to it very much, I can tell you. And now you treasure hunters, since I must go I suggest you come with me. I can help you carry the treasure to my kitbag. I'm going home to have a cat nap as I feel rather tired."

They wrapped their parcels up again. (Though they tried to be careful, they did not make a very neat job of it.) Then they went with Mrs Southerby outside, and down the path that led from her old crumbling house. Marina looked back.

"It must have been a lovely house to live in," she said. "It seems sad, but sad in a *happy* way."

"You're a bit crazy," Timothy declared. "How could it be sad in a happy way. It's like saying you're wet in a dry way."

"Not it isn't!" Marina said hotly, but she couldn't explain what she meant.

Mrs Southerby looked behind her too. "I enjoyed living there," she remarked. "Goodbye to my green growing things until next week-end."

The overgrown hydrangeas closed behind them and in another minute the old house was hidden by its wild tangly garden and its tall trees. But the treasure it had held for so long went with the treasure hunters, some packed into Mrs Southerby's kitbag with the roses and plums, Timothy and Skip carrying a parcel each. Suddenly Marina laughed.

"What is it?" said Skip, puzzled.

"This!" Marina said, holding out their billy. "I was just thinking how hungry I was, and then I remembered our lunch—we haven't even eaten it—no wonder I felt hungry."

"We ate some plums!" Timothy pointed out.

"We've been too busy to eat," Skip answered. As he spoke his fingers tightened and he felt the shape of the ship's bottle in his hand, and smiled triumphantly.

10
A Party at Clancy's Cabin

Of course, though it had been Marina's idea to have a campfire party, Skip was the one who did most of the work arranging it. Early next morning after breakfast he went over to Clancy's house and asked to use the phone. He rang his home and Mr Harrington answered.

"Daddy," Skip said, "we're going to have a party and you and Mum are invited. Would tonight suit you?"

"One moment, Skip!" Mr Harrington said, "I'll ask your mother. . . . Yes, we'd love to come. Make sure you have plenty to eat, because I'm as hungry as a lion, and you know how greedy your mother is. Shall we bring chops? How are you off for food?"

"Well," Skip replied, "could you bring some more bread, and lots of sausages too because there will be rather a lot of us . . . you and the Clancys and a mystery guest."

"Goodness!" Mr Harrington cried. "A dark stranger wearing a mask?"

"No—not a stranger," said Skip with a chuckle. "It's someone you used to know a long time ago, but you haven't seen her for ages."

"Skip, this *is* mysterious," Mr Harrington declared. "Who on earth——" but Skip hung up quickly. He felt it was rude of him, but it would fill his father with curiosity, and that would be a good thing.

Then he rang Mrs Southerby. He heard the phone go *Bing! Bing!* a few times and then Mrs Southerby herself answered. Over the phone her voice sounded lighter and more rustly than ever.

"Come tonight, Skip?" she said. "Of course I can come. I shall enjoy a good campfire party—and, Skip, do make a billy full of tea. I love billy tea and it is years since I had any. I shall go and make something delicious to bring with me."

Skip thought that Mrs Southerby was an excellent sort of person to invite to a campfire tea.

Both the Clancys said that they would come after milking was over. Clancy said how much he was looking forward to the billy tea, which was strange because Mrs Southerby had just said the same thing.

It was a beautiful day with the hot sun spilling everywhere browning the grass still more, and the Harringtons as well. They put on their swimming suits and went up and down the creek bank looking for wood. When they felt too hot they got into the creek and lay down letting the golden water flow over them. It was like a cool hand stroking all the hot stickiness away. By lunch time they had a large pile of wood and pine cones.

That afternoon they made a Maori oven and put potatoes in it to cook for the evening. It was the biggest oven they had ever made and, because they had plenty, the most potatoes they had ever cooked. The oven was made with hot stones and wood embers smouldering in a hole. These were covered with ferns, turfs and even sacks to keep the heat in. The potatoes were between two layers of fern next to the hot stones. It was an uncomfortable job on a hot afternoon, digging the hole, lighting the fire in it and keeping the hungry flames fed until there were lots of embers to use, but at last it was over and sticky, scorched Skip went down to swim, feeling, as he said, like a piece of toast over-cooked on both sides.

At four o'clock Clancy's lazy mild cows wandered past swishing and chewing, and the children began to feel excited. Evening seemed a lot closer as they followed the cows over to the shed, taking a jug with them.

Of course, in the summer the sun was up for a long time and at five o'clock when Mr and Mrs Harrington drove up it was still warm and bright, though in a different way from midday. The shadows stretched their dark arms out from behind every tree and bush and the sunlight was softer. Instead of being dazzling white and hot it was golden and gentle. The hills, dappled with light and shade, seemed gentle too.

"Well," said Mr Harrington, "where's the food? We're hungry, you know. I'm having a ton of sausages sent round on a truck, but I need something to go on with."

"Have an apple!" said Skip with a grin.

"Is that Skip?" Mr Harrington cried. "I thought it was a wild wood ape. You can't hang up the phone now. Tell me who this mystery guest is—tell me at once."

"Wait and see!" was all Skip would say.

Mr Harrington had brought three pounds of sausages and some chops. "That should be plenty," he said. "Did you remember the tomato sauce, Mary?"

Mrs Harrington said she had.

"Well, I married the right woman!" Mr Harrington declared. "I can never remember it myself, even though you make the best tomato sauce in the world. Let's have a look at that fireplace, Skip . . . it won't be big enough for all of us, and a mystery guest too."

Clancy and Mrs Clancy arrived next. Mrs Clancy brought a big tea towel full of scones still warm from the oven and some salty farm butter.

It was getting round about tea time and Mrs Harrington made the children change into clean clothes she had brought with her. Marina was quite glad to wear a dress again instead of shorts, and Mrs Harrington said how lovely it was to have a daughter among all her boys. Mr Harrington was getting impatient.

"Where's the mystery guest?" he cried. "Holding us up at tea time!"

Skip began to feel slightly nervous, but at that moment he heard the chuggling sound of a car engine and a minute later the funny little car that they had seen yesterday came up with Mrs Southerby at the wheel, tooting and waving as she came.

Mr Harrington stared and frowned and then his mouth fell open. "Mrs Southerby!" he yelled. "Great Scott!" And he bounded over to help her out of the car. She was so small beside him that he lifted her up as if she were a feather to look at her more closely.

"Well, Little Esmond!" she said. "You're not so little these days, are you?"

"Dad was *really* surprised!" Skip said with great satisfaction.

Mr Harrington and Clancy were both talking to Mrs Southerby at the same time, and she was laughing and shaking their hands and even crying a little bit too, because she was so pleased to see them. So the party began—and it was a wonderful party. It smelt wonderful, and it tasted wonderful. Everyone thought so, even Treasure the dog who got in everyone's way. They cooked sausages and chops and ate them in their fingers with baked buttery potatoes. Of course, they got in a mess, but that was what they had expected. They ate the good salad that Mrs Harrington had brought and Mrs Clancy's scones, and big pieces of Mrs Southerby's chocolate cake. They all talked and laughed, and Mrs Southerby and the children kept on smiling secretly at each other because they knew there was more to come.

By the time everyone was sitting around with cups of billy tea, tasting faintly of summer grass and wood smoke, it was dark, and the only light there was came from the fire. It was then that Skip, Marina and Timothy brought out their treasure in its parcels and the clue they had found in Clancy's cabin, and put it down at Mr Harrington's feet.

"What's this, kids?" he said. "Christmas again already?"

"This is *our* joke, Daddy," Marina replied, grinning.

Mr Harrington picked up the paper with the pattern and the rhyme on it first. His mouth fell open for the second time that evening, and he gave the children and Mrs Southerby a sharp glance across the smouldering fire. He looked very like Skip for a moment. For once he didn't say a word until he had opened all his parcels and Clancy had opened his. Each present made Mr Harrington look more serious than ever. At last he said,

"I can see you've had some adventures. Tell me all about it quickly."

So they told him the whole story . . . how Skip had found the pattern and the rhyme in Clancy's cabin, how they had worked it out and followed the old road to Mrs Southerby's house, how they had met Mrs Southerby there and she had told them the history of the treasure hunt, and how Timothy had found the treasure in the old globe of the world.

". . . so you see, Daddy," ended Marina, "it's not Christmas. It's your birthday."

Mr Harrington looked at Clancy and Mrs Southerby,

and the children knew that these three were remembering the good old days they had shared, and Big Esmond who had hidden the treasure. Then Mr Harrington said,

"You know—I think I've grown a bit old for most of these birthday presents." He smiled at Timothy's hopeful face. "Of course, they're not new, but if you'd like the dagger, Tim, and you the ship, Skipper, and if you'd like the little picture, Marina, you can have them." Marina threw her arms around his neck to hug him. "Here, you'll upset my billy tea!" cried Mr Harrington anxiously.

"As for me," Clancy said, "I've read this book before. You'd better have it. Pity to split up the treasure." And he gave them the copy of *Treasure Island*.

The children thanked him, and Marina, looking round the circle of faces, thought it was the most wonderful evening she had ever spent—firelight, Treasure the dog, old friends reunited, and a treasure all to themselves . . . these things were mixed together to make a really special evening, one to remember for ever.

She caught her mother's eye and smiled happily.

Mr Harrington got to his feet. "I'm going to make a speech!" he cried. "I want you all to drink a toast with what is left of your billy tea to my three clever children who found the treasure, and to the memory of my grandfather Big Esmond who hid it so well."

Then the Clancys and Mr and Mrs Harrington and Mrs Southerby cheered and cheered, and drank some of their hot billy tea.

Skip and Timothy, flickery in the firelight, blushed and grinned and pretended to look at sore places on their knees. Marina, however, said seriously,

"I think it ought to be a toast to the one who kept the secret so long . . . Clancy's cabin over there."

Mr Harrington laughed. "My word, yes! A toast to Clancy's cabin! We had some great times there, Clancy. May people who like camping out and treasure hunts have many more."

Everyone cheered, and dog Treasure barked, until the echoes sounded, and they drank their billy tea until it was all gone, while Clancy's cabin, dim and shadowy in its moss and ferns, seemed to blink at the fire and suddenly banged its door as if it were cheering too.